AJ AND THE MAGIC KITE

Written by Crystal Senter-Brown

Illustrated by Janice Treece-Senter

© 2017 Crystal Senter-Brown, Janice Treece-Senter

For exclusive content or to join the author's mailing list, visit
www.crystalsenterbrown.com.

For school appearances, speaking engagements and more, email the author at
gabbygirlmedia@gmail.com.

Download free worksheets, coloring pages and more at
www.ajandthemagickite.com.

For Adonté Jerome ("AJ")

There once was a boy named AJ.

He lived in a town called Blue, which was deep in the mountains of Virginia.

It was very beautiful there.

The grass was always green, and there were lots of animals there!

But AJ didn't like to go to school.
The children often made fun of him
because his skin was brown.

They also told AJ
that African-American people
were worthless.

When AJ told his Mom and Dad,
they told him he should
be proud to be brown!

One afternoon, AJ sat at the kitchen table
to do his homework.
AJ put his head down on the table and
before long, he fell fast asleep!

Soon, AJ heard a knock at the door.

"Who is it?" AJ asked.

"Your new friend Jerome," the voice answered.

AJ opened the door to find
a young boy holding a kite.

Rubbing his eyes, AJ asked: "Why are you here?"
"I have something I want to show you,"
Jerome said,
"but we have to fly to get there."

"Fly? What do you mean fly? How?"
Before AJ could finish his sentence, Jerome took
AJ's hand and yanked on the kite string.

Suddenly, AJ heard a loud
WOOOOOOOOOOOSH sound,
and soon, they were in the air!

They flew up,
up,
up!

They soared even higher than the birds!

At first AJ was little afraid because he had never been so high in the sky before!

But after a few minutes, AJ thought it was pretty cool to fly and he loved the view from way up high!

"Are you ready to land?"
Jerome asked AJ a few minutes later.

"Yes!" AJ said.

"Hold on!" Jerome yelled.

Soon, they landed in front of a very tall building.

"My friend Corey lives in a tall building just like this one!" AJ said. "We have to take the elevator to get to his apartment."

"Then you should be very happy that African-American inventor James Cooper was born, because he invented a device that helped to make the elevator better," Jerome said.

"Boy, am I glad that we have elevators! I remember one time my friend's elevator was broken and we had to walk up ten flights of stairs!"

"Wow!" Jerome said. "Hey! Look down there!"

In the valley below,
there was a car accident.

AJ could see that one driver
was *really* upset, and he was
waving his arms at the other driver.

"Where is the traffic light?"
AJ asked Jerome.

"The traffic was invented
by Garrett A. Morgan,
an African-American inventor,"
Jerome said.

"That driver sure looks mad!" AJ said.

"I bet he wishes there were African-American inventions," Jerome laughed.
"Are you ready for our next stop?"

"Yep!" AJ said.

Within seconds, the boys
were standing in a kitchen
where a family was eating dinner-
on the floor!

There was no kitchen table,
and dirt was scattered
all over the kitchen floor.

"Why is the kitchen
such a mess? And where is the
kitchen table?" AJ asked Jerome.

"Well, the dustpan and the kitchen
table were invented by
African-Americans," Jerome said.

"No way!" AJ said.

"Yes!" Jerome said.

"Let's get out of here!" AJ said.

AJ reached for the doorknob,
but it was gone!

"Where is the doorknob?"
AJ asked Jerome.

"O. Dorsey invented the doorknob,
but remember, we have magic!"
Jerome said as he held up the kite.

"But I don't think
I like *this* world," AJ said.
"Can we go back to *my* world?"
he asked.

"Sure!" Jerome said,
and with a wink of his eye,
the boys were standing
inside AJ's front door.

Jerome turned to AJ and said:
"I have to go now, but don't forget
what I showed you today.
And remember, you come from a
long line of smart African-American
people who made a
big difference in our world!"

"I'll remember!" AJ said.

Later that night, AJ went to his dresser to find
pajamas for bed, and guess
what was in his room?

The magic kite!

There was a note attached to the kite that read:
*"Tomorrow, when the children begin to make fun of
you, remember what I showed you today."*

And the next day, when the children made fun
of AJ, it didn't bother him. Instead, he stood
proudly as he remembered what he learned
from Jerome the day before!

Activities

AJ and the Magic Kite Word Search

```
                    S P
                  Y O R I
                V P Y K Q K
              K Q N B C H W R
            G U E D O M X T P D
          V D E Q W Q T B A N R R
        I G R M L T L Z E L A C E Q
      F P G B G R F A M I L Y W P D Y
    N A D F D I V U A O E O P J F L Z P
  W I B V M D W Z Z G L N K K C C V L B B
X T L C C K I T E B V R I B V Z Z V U D
  S U A K H B M A K O Q S N Z X V B S
    E W Q Q B T R O V C W K B B N G
      V H T B D L K D O Y B Y A C
        R G Y F B R R F L Y E G
          G E T F B B W X T U
            Z D P F B U F V
              F O C O W U
                U M Y C
                  K L
```

SKY
KITE
BROWN
NOTE
BLUE
DIRT
FLOOR
TALL
TABLE
FLY
FAMILY
GREEN
BOY

AJ and the Magic Kite Word Scramble

Name: _____

Please unscramble the words below

1. EIKT _____

2. UELB _____

3. YFL _____

4. YSK _____

5. IDTR _____

6. TLAL _____

7. ORFOL _____

8. EABTL _____

9. YFLIAM _____

10. EOTN _____

11. WRNBO _____

Words: SKY, KITE, BROWN, NOTE, BLUE, DIRT, FLOOR, TALL, TABLE, FLY, FAMILY

If YOU had a magic kite, where would you fly to?
Draw a picture!

Draw and color the items that were invented (or improved upon) by an African-American

Dust pan	Kitchen Table

Doorknob	Stoplight

Color your own magic kite!

About the Author:

Crystal Senter-Brown (daughter) is an award-winning writer who has been featured in Redbook Magazine, Vibe Magazine and Essence Magazine. She has been a performance poet and writer for most of her life. Born in Morristown, TN to a bass-playing Baptist preacher (Dad) and a visual artist/ painter (Mom), Crystal performed her first poem onstage at the age of six.

She is the author of seven books: *AJ and the Magic Kite, Gabby Gives Back, But Now I See, But You Have Such a Pretty Face*, Doubledutch, *Gabby Saturday* and *The Rhythm in Blue*, which was turned into a feature film. She is an adjunct professor and lives in New England with her husband Corey, son Adonté and a maniac puppy named Venus. Visit Crystal online at www.crystalsenterbrown.com.

About the Illustrator:

Janice Treece- Senter (mother) was born in East Tennessee and has since lived throughout the Southeast as a fine artist and an artist educational consultant. Self-taught, Janice has worked with some of the best and brightest fine artists across the United States.

Her work has appeared internationally on the hit ABC television show "Extreme Home Makeover" and she has received numerous awards for her art. She has also designed book covers for over 20 books. Visit Janice online at www.janicetreecesenter.com.

Made in the USA
Monee, IL
23 May 2022

96269040R00020